P9-APX-489

Bobcat Rescue

Susan Hughes

Illustrations by Heather Graham

SCHOLASTIC CANADA LTD.
Toronto New York London Auckland Sydney
Mexico City New Delhi Hong Kong Buenos Aires

Scholastic Canada Ltd.
604 King Street West, Toronto, Ontario M5V 1E1, Canada

Scholastic Inc.
557 Broadway, New York, NY 10012, USA

Scholastic Australia Pty Limited
PO Box 579, Gosford, NSW 2250, Australia

Scholastic New Zealand Limited
Private Bag 94407, Botany, Manukau 2163, New Zealand

Scholastic Children's Books
Euston House, 24 Eversholt Street, London NW1 1DB, UK

www.scholastic.ca

National Library of Canada Cataloguing in Publication

Hughes, Susan, 1960-
Bobcat rescue / Susan Hughes ; illustrations by Heather Graham.

(Wild paws)

Originally publ. 2003.

ISBN 978-0-545-98525-3

I. Graham, Heather II. Title. III. Series : Hughes, Susan, 1960- . Wild paws.
PS8565.U42B62 2009   jC813'.54   C2009-901182-4

ISBN-10 0-545-98525-0

Text copyright © 2003 by Susan Hughes
Cover photo copyright © Firstlight/Victoria Hurst
Illustrations copyright © Scholastic Canada Ltd.
All rights reserved.

No part of this publication may be reproduced or stored in a retrieval system, or transmitted in any form or by any means, electronic, mechanical, recording, or otherwise, without written permission of the publisher, Scholastic Canada Ltd., 604 King Street West, Toronto, Ontario M5V 1E1, Canada. In the case of photocopying or other reprographic copying, a licence must be obtained from Access Copyright (Canadian Copyright Licensing Agency), 1 Yonge Street, Suite 800, Toronto, Ontario M5E 1E5 (1-800-893-5777).

6 5 4 3 2   Printed in Canada   121   14 15 16 17 18

MIX
Paper from
responsible sources
FSC
www.fsc.org   FSC® C004071

To my darling daughter, Sophie.

I would like to thank Evelyn Davis, volunteer at the Wildlife Education and Rehabilitation Center in Morgan Hill, California, for providing me with detailed information about WERC's innovative method of raising baby bobcats with the help of costumed "foster moms." Thanks also to Hope Swinimer, director of the Eastern Shore Wildlife Rehabilitation Centre in Seaforth, Nova Scotia, for reviewing the manuscript for accuracy.

Contents

Chapter One

School Tomorrow

Max Kearney sighed. She kicked at the stones on the forest path.

"What's wrong?" asked her younger brother David.

Max and David were on a hike with their grandmother. It had been a short drive to the woods from their new home in the village of Maple Hill. At the beginning of their walk, David had spotted a red-winged blackbird, and Grandma had pointed out flowers like bunchberry and lady's slipper. But Max had been too anxious to enjoy these signs of summer.

Max stuffed her hands deep into the pockets of

her shorts and sighed again. "Oh, you know," she replied. "Just thinking about school tomorrow."

David nodded. He looked at Max, and then he heaved a big sigh too.

Max grinned at that. She knew her brother was trying to make her feel better. She knew he couldn't wait to go to grade two at their new school. He couldn't wait to meet new kids and make some friends before summer started.

"Too bad we had to leave the city and come here," David added. He did a good job of making his voice sound sad and disappointed. He even kicked at some stones, just as Max had done.

Max stopped. She put her hands on her hips and looked at David.

"Do you remember when we had the vote?" Max said.

David nodded.

Their parents had always wanted to move away from the city. When they discovered the village of Maple Hill, it seemed just right. Mom could still work at her same job, and Dad could find a job in the town just north of Maple Hill.

If they moved to Maple Hill, they could get a house. There would be enough room for Grandma to come and live with them too. Grandma loved the countryside. She was always reading books about forest creatures, and she liked to walk in the woods and take pictures. Max adored the animal stories Grandma shared with her. Grandma said that Max seemed to love nature as much as she did.

Max looked down the path. Grandma had stopped to take a photo of new blossoms on a branch.

"We both voted to come," Max recalled. "Didn't we?"

"Yes," David agreed.

"And it's fine. The village is fine. But I'm worried about school. There's only a few weeks before it ends for the summer. What if I don't make friends quickly? I'll be . . . " Max sighed. "I'll be lonely all summer long."

Max reached down and picked up some pebbles. Then she dropped them, one by one, on the path. "All the kids in my new class have probably known each other for years — for all their lives! They probably won't even want to make another friend."

Max and David's family had moved to Maple Hill just last week. Their parents said they could wait until Monday to start school. Tomorrow was Monday, but now Max wished they had started school the very first day they arrived.

Max felt a worried knot in her stomach. She thought of the long summer months stretching ahead. Could she make new friends in time to enjoy her vacation?

She could see that David was trying to look grim, even though he was thrilled to be living in a new town. Even though it was almost summer, his favourite time of year. Even though he liked meeting new kids. David pulled his mouth down. He wrinkled his eyebrows. He folded his arms.

Max looked carefully at her brother. Her brown eyes started to sparkle. She could tell David was trying not to smile.

"David, stop it," Max told him, grinning.

He tried even harder to look serious.

Max began to laugh. "You love it here!" she reminded him.

David's mask fell away. His face was shining with happiness.

"You love the fields and the fresh air!" cried Max.

"Well, *you* love exploring these paths in the woods!" David yelled.

It was Max's turn. "*You* love our little house on a quiet street!"

"*You* love having Grandma stay with us!" David shouted.

With a whoop, Max tagged David. Her ponytail swung behind her.

"Catch me if you can!" she challenged him, running off between the trees. It was true, Max thought as she sprinted along. She did love all those things about their new home. Everything would be fine – as long as she could make some friends here.

Sure, David was OK to hang around with. As OK as any little brother could be. But Max needed a real friend of her own. Someone her age. Someone who liked animals as much as she did. Even though the thought of making a new friend scared her. Even though Max worried that she wasn't very good at it.

She gulped. What if no one here liked her?

Max continued running, making up her own path. She twisted and turned around the tree trunks and jumped from one grey rock to another. She went just fast enough that David could keep up, but not tag her back.

Finally the trees ended and Max reached a clearing. She walked across it, panting, and then stopped at the foot of a rocky cliff, not wanting to go further and get lost.

She bent over, her hands on her knees, taking some deep breaths.

Then all of a sudden, Max stood up straight.
Her eyes opened wide.
"What was that?" she whispered.

Chapter Two

The Sound in the Woods

"Gotcha!" puffed David, tagging Max's arm. He had finally caught up to her.

Max put a finger to her lips. "Shhh," she warned.

Max and David stood quietly.

Then they both heard the faint noise.

Mew-mew-mew.

Mew-mew-mew.

Max and her brother looked at each other.

"What is it?" asked David softly.

Max listened intently.

"It sure sounds like a kitten," she said, puzzled. "But how could that be? How could a cat be out here in the middle of nowhere?"

In these woods, there were no houses or farms around.

"I think it's coming from over there," David said.

Max moved slowly toward a big pile of rocks at the bottom of the cliff. David followed behind.

Mew-mew.

The sound grew louder and more plaintive. Max knew they were heading in the right direction. When she reached the rocks, she started across them carefully, placing each foot just so. Teetering slightly, she had to grasp at the rocks for balance.

Mew-mew.

Max stopped so suddenly that David bumped right into her.

"Sorry," he said. But his sister wasn't listening.

"Look," she said, pointing.

There, under a rocky ledge, was a small shape. It was moving.

"Ohhhh," whispered David. "It *is* a kitten!"

They moved closer to get a better look. Max squatted low and peered between the rocks.

Yes, it certainly did look like a kitten. A very young kitten. Its fur was orangey-brown, dappled with black and white. It had wide paws with tiny sharp claws. The kitten huddled close to the rock, but its head turned from side to side while it cried.

"Look, its eyes are still shut!" said Max. "Remember when Amanda's cat, Matilda, had babies? Their eyes were shut when they were born too!"

"This kitten looks like it doesn't have any ears," pointed out David. "But it does. Look! It's holding them flat against its head, like a little furry seal pup!"

"Oh, and look at its tiny orangish nose and its tiny sad mouth," Max added. "But where's its tail?"

"Maybe it's lying on it," suggested David.

"Poor little thing," said Max, soothingly. "What are you doing out here in the rocks? Why are you out in the middle of the woods?"

Max looked around the clearing. There was no sign of a mother cat.

"Maybe we should try to help it," said Max. She couldn't wait to touch the kitten's soft fur. She couldn't wait to pick it up and comfort it in her arms.

"Good idea," said David. "We can take it home and feed it."

Slowly Max leaned forward. She reached into the opening between the rocks.

But just then, they heard, "Stop!"

Chapter Three

Radio Report

It was Grandma. She stood at the edge of the clearing, wiping her brow.

"Stop!" she repeated.

"But Grandma, we've found a kitten . . . " David began to say.

Max watched as Grandma cautiously made her way around a few rocks. But then she stopped.

"I can't get any closer," she said, "but I think I can see from here . . . " Grandma craned her neck toward where the children were pointing. "Oh, I can see," she crooned. "It's so tiny."

Mew-mew-mew.

"Grandma, listen!" Max said. "The kitten is crying

again! It must be really hungry! Why did you tell us to stop? Can't we pick it up?" Max could hardly stand it. She could almost feel the soft body of the kitten in her arms. She imagined the little face pressed against her cheek.

"I know you want to help it, Max," Grandma said. "But there are a few important things you need to know. Especially now that we are living in the country. Especially now that we are living where the wild things make their homes too."

Max and David carefully climbed back over the rocks to hear what Grandma had to say. They perched on a nearby boulder.

"First, we always have to try to think about what's best for the animal," Grandma explained. "Not all baby animals that are alone have been abandoned. Sometimes their moms have to go and get food for their babies. They can't be with them all the time."

Max nodded. Grandma had told her stories about this happening many times. "The mother takes better care of her babies than any human could," she agreed, smiling. "So maybe the kitten's mother will come back and take care of her baby after all!"

Mew-mew-mew.

Max turned back and looked at the helpless kitten.

"But Grandma, we can't just leave without knowing," said Max. She spread her arms wide. "Listen to it mewing so sadly. We can't just leave without knowing for sure that its mother will come back."

"I agree," nodded Grandma.

"So how can you tell?" asked Max. "How can you tell if a mother is going to come back?"

Grandma stood up and brushed off her pants. "To know if a baby is really abandoned, you usually have to watch for several hours. I think that's about how long mothers can be away from their babies."

"Well, that's what we'll do then," Max decided. "We'll just have to wait here until this kitten's mother comes back."

"Right," David agreed.

But Grandma was still looking toward the little kitten. She had a funny look on her face, as if she wasn't certain about something. As if she was still thinking about the situation. It gave Max butterflies in her stomach.

"What is it, Grandma?" she asked.

Grandma reached over and took their hands. "I

heard some sad news on the radio this morning. A mother bobcat was hit by a car on a road near here."

"A bobcat?" repeated David. "I didn't know there were bobcats around here!"

"Neither did I," admitted Grandma. "They are very private animals. They usually only come out at night. People hardly ever catch sight of them."

Max shook her head. The news *was* sad. But what did it have to do with them? Unless . . .

"What else, Grandma?" Max asked, looking at her intently.

"The mother had a baby with her. The local wildlife authority thinks that maybe she was trying to move her babies to a safer place. Maybe she thought she was living too close to humans." Grandma paused. "The baby was killed too."

"Oh, no," Max moaned.

"But," Grandma went on, "most bobcats give birth to at least two babies. So it makes sense that there might be another bobcat kitten around." Max felt Grandma squeeze her hand. "If there is, it's probably hungry and cold and crying for its mother."

Max looked toward the rocks.

Then she looked back at her grandmother, her eyes wide.

Could it possibly be?

Chapter Four

Tuffy

"Grandma," Max said. "Do you think . . . do you think *this* kitten is a bobcat kitten?"

"What?" David looked back and forth from Max to Grandma. "But this is a baby cat. It's the kitten of someone's pet cat . . . Isn't it?"

Grandma laid her hands gently on the children's shoulders.

"I think Max is right. I think you've found the other baby bobcat. Max, I can see the kitten from here, but not very well. Go and take a really close look. Tell me what the kitten's tail looks like."

Max moved out from under Grandma's hands. She made her way back to the rock opening as quickly as she could. Then she crouched down.

The baby animal was scrunching up its little face. It began to mew again. Max looked intently. The kitten *wasn't* lying on its tail, like David had thought.

"Wow! The kitten's tail is really short," Max called over her shoulder. "It's stubby."

Grandma nodded. "A bobtail," she said.

"So this *must* be a baby bobcat," Max whispered to herself. This was a *bobcat kitten!*

Max had so many questions. But she asked the most important one first. "So it's OK to help it, Grandma? Now that we know it's all alone?" Max looked at her with pleading eyes.

"I think it's important that we be absolutely certain," Grandma said thoughtfully. "We want to do what's best for the kitten." Grandma took off her knapsack. She found a pencil and opened a small pad of paper. Then she pulled out her cell phone and pressed some buttons.

"Could I have the number of the veterinary clinic in Maple Hill, please?"

Grandma wrote down a phone number and then pressed more numbers.

While she spoke, Max gazed at the tiny, soft kitten. She heard Grandma describing it — its closed eyes, its orangey-brown fur, its bobbed tail. Then she heard her say, "Thank you, Dr. Sweeny. I understand. Goodbye."

"It's just as I thought," she reported sadly as Max scrambled over to hear the news. "Dr. Sweeny knows a lot about dogs and cats and not much about wild animals. But when he heard me describe it, he seemed certain that this was a baby bobcat. He also felt that it must have been this baby's mother that was killed. There just aren't that many bobcats around here."

No one spoke for a moment.

Then Max stood up, a glimmer in her eye. "Its mother isn't coming back, but *we're* here. Did the vet say we should leave it . . . or can we take it home and try to help it?"

Grandma smiled. "The vet says the kitten needs to be rescued. We'll take it with us, but we won't be taking it home. Dr. Sweeny told me about a wild animal clinic just outside the village. It's called Wild Paws and Claws. Dr. Sweeney thinks they may be able to help this little creature there."

Max sighed with relief.

"And Dr. Sweeny told me what we should do now. Let's see here . . . " Grandma reached into her backpack and pulled out a heavy sweater. She hesitated for a minute, then said, "I think you can manage this, Max."

Max reached out to take the sweater from her. "Just be very careful to cover the kitten completely with the sweater. It may be little, but its claws will be sharp."

Max nodded, feeling her heart race. It was a huge responsibility.

She approached the rocks quietly. She saw the baby bobcat just as it began to mew again. Carefully, Max reached between the rocks, holding the sweater open wide. Then she wrapped it gently around the tiny body of the kitten. The little animal didn't even struggle. In fact, it stopped crying right away. It was as if it was comforted by the touch.

Max brought the bobcat into her arms. The kitten was very light — not even as heavy as a paperback book. As she gingerly made her way back to Grandma and David, Max held the bobcat close and murmured, "There we go. It's OK. We'll take care of you."

Only the bobcat's head was poking out from the sweater. Its ears were still flat against its head. A beautiful ruff of fur framed its tiny face. Gently, Max touched the soft fur on the top of the kitten's head with her fingertips. David reached over and stroked it too. Grandma smiled.

"OK," Max instructed. "Let's head out."

She and David took turns carrying the kitten until they had returned to the car.

"Look," Max said to David. The tiny bobcat had stopped wiggling. It had fallen asleep during the walk, comforted by their gentle arms and the warmth of their bodies.

Max and David sat in the back seat, side by side, with the small kitten in Max's lap.

Max asked, "Can we go right now? To the wildlife clinic?"

"Of course we can," Grandma said. "We want to get that bobcat kitty taken care of, don't we?"

Max nodded.

"The clinic is on Hare Bell Lane," Grandma told them as she put the car into gear. She passed the map back to Max. "Perhaps you could find it for me, and give me directions."

Max found the local road quickly. "It's really close to our house!" she exclaimed. "It's even close enough to walk to from there!"

As they drove along, Max sneaked another peek at the kitten. She admired its tiny claws. They did look very sharp! Max carefully wrapped them back up in the sweater. Every so often, Max reached down and brushed the bobcat's fur with her fingers.

The kitten was so small! It was so dainty! But it would have to be tough to survive without its mom, thought Max.

"Hey, look," David said. He lightly touched the tip of one of the bobcat's ears. "Aren't its ears pointy?"

Max could see that they were.

"And they have little tufts on them," Max pointed out. Then she had an idea. "Hey, maybe that would be a good name for the bobcat. Tuffy. Because of the tufts, and because this kitty will have to be tough to make it on its own. Get it? Tuffy?"

David smiled and nodded.

"Perfect," Grandma said from the front seat.

Only a few twists and turns later, they saw a sign ahead: *Wild Paws and Claws Clinic and Rehabilitation*

Centre. Below the words was a drawing of a paw print.

"This is it!" Max said. "I sure hope they can help Tuffy here!"

"Well, we'll find out soon enough," Grandma said, turning into the stony driveway.

Chapter Five

Whooo Are You?

"What is *rehabilitation*?" David asked, sounding out the word he had seen on the sign.

Max explained. "I've read about it in some of Gran's books. If this is a rehabilitation centre, it means that they don't just treat the injured animals here. They also look after them while they get better from their injuries."

"David and I will wait here with Tuffy," Grandma suggested, after she parked the car.

"All right," Max said. Everyone got out of the car, and Max carefully handed the bundled kitten to Grandma. Then she hurried toward the small building. At the front door, a smaller sign showed the same paw print and the word *Office*. The door was slightly open.

Max paused at the top of the building's stairs. Would anyone be able to help? she wondered. Then she knocked once on the door and called, "Hello?"

No one answered.

Max knew Tuffy needed help. She knew she had to find whoever was in charge. Taking a deep breath, she pushed the door open and walked in.

From the hallway, Max could see three doors. The two on the left were closed. The one open door on the right led to an office. Max could see a bookcase stuffed with magazines, books and loose papers. An open drawer in a filing cabinet was overflowing with folders. She walked down the hall and peered inside the door. A desk was piled high with papers, and behind the desk sat a woman with her face in her hands. She was crying. Max gulped. She forced herself to tap on the open door. She had no choice. There didn't seem to be anyone else around to ask for help.

At the sound of Max's knock, the woman looked up. She cocked her head to one side and peered at Max. Then she rubbed briskly at her eyes. She put on a pair of glasses with round frames. She peered at Max again.

"Whooo are you?" she asked. At another time, Max would have grinned. But not now. She was too worried. Worried about Tuffy, and worried by this woman's tears.

"I'm . . . I'm Max," she said.

"And how can I help you, Max?" said the woman. She blew her nose with a loud snort. Then she craned her neck forward and stuck her chin out.

"Well . . . " Max hesitated. She wished she wasn't here. She wished she hadn't seen the woman crying. She wanted to turn and run.

But then she thought about Tuffy. She knew that this woman might be able to help.

"Well, you see, we found a baby bobcat today. At least, Grandma thinks it's a bobcat. She heard on the radio that a mother had been killed — "

Before she could say more, the woman leaped to her feet. Max barely had time to marvel at how tall and thin she was. And then the woman was at her side.

"Why didn't you say so at once, dear?" she said briskly. "Where is the bobcat?"

Max didn't even get a chance to answer. The woman was already leading the way out the front door.

When she spotted the bundle in Grandma's

arms, the woman hurried over with great long strides.

"Is this the bobcat kitten?" she asked, holding out her hands.

"Yes," Max heard Grandma say. "It's – "

"Let me see," the woman said. Before Max had even reached the car, the woman was holding the bobcat and had taken a quick look at it. "Well, I don't know a lot about bobcats. Never had one here before. But this one is a female, that much I know. We need to get her warm and keep her quiet. Then she'll need to be looked at by my wildlife vet."

Abruptly, she spun on her heel and, with the bobcat in her arms, swiftly headed back toward the office. Max, David and Grandma were speechless as they watched her go.

Just as she was about to disappear through the door, the woman turned her head. She called back loudly over her shoulder, "Abigail Abernathy. That's my name. You can call me Abbie. Nice to meet you. Come back tomorrow."

And then Abbie and Tuffy were gone.

Chapter Six

First Day

Max stood beside her new teacher at the front of the class. Ms Nickel put her hand kindly on Max's shoulder.

"Class, this is Maxine Kearney," Ms Nickel said. Max tried not to blush as all the students looked at her.

"Maxine, this is Sarah," Ms Nickel told Max as she pointed at another girl. "Sarah will be your special friend today in Room 108."

Sarah had two long red braids and freckles across her nose. She smiled at Max, and Max smiled back. The teacher probably told Sarah to be friendly to the new girl, Max thought.

"Sarah, will you take Maxine out into the hall and show her where her coat hook is?" Ms Nickel asked.

Max followed Sarah out of the classroom.

"This is your hook, Maxine," said Sarah. "It's right beside mine."

Max hung up her jacket. "Thanks," she said. "And by the way, my name is Maxine, but you can call me Max."

Suddenly, Abigail Abernathy popped into Max's head. *You can call me Abbie*, the woman had said.

Max froze in the middle of hanging up her jacket. She was very worried about Tuffy. How was the bobcat kitten? Abbie said she had never cared for a bobcat before. Had she been able to feed her?

Her smile faded. Maybe Tuffy wouldn't survive without her mother.

Max felt her eyes begin to sting. She turned her head and tried to blink her tears away. What if Sarah made fun of her?

But then she felt Sarah's hand gently tap her shoulder. She heard Sarah ask, "Are you OK? Are you nervous because it's your first day at this school?"

Max turned to the girl. Sarah gave her a little

awkward grin, like she wasn't sure how to make Max feel better.

"Oh, it's not that," Max replied slowly. And to her surprise, it was true. She could hardly think about anything but Tuffy.

"What is it, then?" asked Sarah. Her blue eyes were wide and seemed full of concern.

Quickly Max told her all about finding the baby bobcat and taking her to the Wild Paws and Claws clinic. "And when my brother and I got back home, we told our parents all about Tuffy. We all went to the computer and looked up information about bobcats. They can be found between central

Mexico and southern Canada!"

"Wow! I never knew there were bobcats in Canada," Sarah marvelled. "What else did you find out?"

"Well, we learned that bobcats only eat meat — mostly small birds and other animals. They have smallish feet and shortish legs, so they don't like deep snow. That's why they don't live in northern Canada. And it *is* possible to raise a baby bobcat and then return it to the wild. It's possible, but it doesn't always work . . . " Max's voice went quiet.

Sarah spoke quickly. "Tell me again: what does Tuffy look like?" she prompted Max.

An image of Tuffy came into Max's head, and she couldn't help but smile. "Tuffy is so cute, Sarah. She's tiny — a little orangey-brown spotted fluffball. She has a short tail, a bobbed tail. That's how the bobcat gets its name. Her face has a beautiful ruff of fur around it, and she has little eyes that are closed tight. Her ears have little tufts on the tops."

Then Max's smile vanished again. "Tuffy is so little," she confided to Sarah. "She's so little, and she doesn't have her mom to feed her anymore. I'm not sure if she's going to be all right. As soon as school is over, I'm going to the wildlife centre to check on her."

Ms Nickel appeared in the doorway. "I see you girls are going to be good friends," she said.

Max was surprised. She had forgotten all about making a new friend, but maybe it had already happened.

"Now it's time to come back in and rejoin the others!" Ms Nickel said.

The girls followed their teacher back inside and she showed Max to her new desk. It was right beside Sarah's.

Max tried to catch Sarah's eye. Finally, Sarah looked over at her. Max whispered to her, "Do you want to come with me to see Tuffy after school?"

Sarah's eyes shone. "OK," she agreed, grinning. "I'll ask my mom at lunch."

The morning sped by. At recess, Max saw David playing with a small group of grade two boys. He waved happily at her and she waved back.

At lunchtime, Max and David met outside the school fence and walked home together. David couldn't stop talking about the new friend he had made. Max just listened with a smile. She didn't even try to tell him about Sarah.

Grandma had sandwiches and soup waiting for them. Max ate up quickly so she could spend the rest of her lunch hour on the Internet. There was still so much to learn about bobcats!

"Wow, listen to this, Grandma," Max called. "*Bobcat kittens are often born in caves or inside hollow logs. Sometimes a mother makes a den between rocks.*"

"Just like Tuffy's mom did," David pointed out.

Max read on: "*A mother bobcat often has one to four babies in the spring. They are tiny and helpless. They can't see or hear, but they can smell! When bobcat kittens are about two weeks old, their eyes begin to open. Their ears begin to unfold.*"

Max concluded, "So Tuffy must be less than two weeks old."

She continued to read from the screen. "*A bobcat is a mammal. Like every mammal, a baby bobcat drinks milk from its mother. Without this milk, a baby bobcat wouldn't survive.*"

There was silence.

Max and David looked at each other.

Grandma had come into the room. She was listening too. "Don't worry," she said soothingly. "I'm sure Abigail is doing a fine job with Tuffy. And when Max goes over there this afternoon she can find out all about it."

"But Grandma," David began anxiously. "How can Abigail feed Tuffy? What will she give the bobcat to drink?"

"Hey, look," interrupted Max. Her voice was cheerful and bright. "Look. Right here on this website. It says that there's a rehabilitation centre that specializes in bobcats. The centre is in the western United States, and it even gives the phone number." She picked up the phone. "I'm going to phone Abbie with this number. The people at this centre might help her find out how to care for Tuffy!"

Max quickly made the call. Abbie wasn't there, but Max left the information on the Wild Paws and Claws answering machine.

Chapter Seven

Goodbye, Dr. Jacobs

After lunch, David and Max reached the playground quickly. Right away, Sarah came running over. She smiled at Max and said, "Hi."

"Hi, Sarah," answered Max. "So, what did your mother say? Can you come to the clinic with me? Do you still want to?" She smiled brightly at Sarah. Behind her back, she crossed the fingers of one hand.

Sarah's eyes lit up. "I'd love to come. My mom said yes, as long as I'm home by supper." Then the bell rang, and the girls headed for the school doors together.

To Max, the afternoon seemed to pass slowly, even though it was her first day in a new class. But finally it was 3:30, and school let out for the day.

Max and Sarah set out directly for Wild Paws and Claws.

Sarah did a little skip. "I've never been there before," she exclaimed. "It sounds like a really interesting place to visit." Then she said, "You know, when I asked my mother if I could come here with you, she said, 'Oh, is Wild Paws and Claws still open?' She heard a shopkeeper in town complaining that its bill for bird food hadn't been paid."

"Hmm," Max pondered. "Well, it's still open, all right." But she told Sarah how she had found Abbie crying at her desk a day earlier. Maybe this was why.

The two girls walked in silence for a moment. Then Max cried, "There it is!" as she saw the sign by the road. "See the paw prints on the sign, Sarah?"

Sarah nodded happily as they passed through the gate.

"We didn't get a chance to see much when we were here yesterday. None of the animals anyway," Max admitted. "We were mostly concerned with getting Tuffy looked after."

"I hope we can look around today," said Sarah. The girls headed down the long driveway and were soon standing at the front door of the office.

Max knocked once on the door, then twice. No one answered. She knocked again, harder. Still no answer.

Max and Sarah looked at each other.

"Now what?" Sarah asked.

"Let's go around back," suggested Max. "Maybe Abbie is outside somewhere."

They walked around the small building. Behind it, they saw a large grove of trees, and a path leading into it.

As they followed the path, they began to hear sounds. Excited sounds. Excited animal sounds. Max, the leader, began walking faster.

But she stopped when she entered a wide clearing. Sunlight poured down through the trees on a large circle of animal pens.

"Oh, look!" cried Sarah. In one pen, there was a fox with a bushy tail. He was yipping and prancing about.

Max moved closer to take a better look.

"He only has three legs," Sarah said. "But he's beautiful. Look at the white fur on the tip of his tail!"

After admiring the fox, the girls went on to the next pen.

"This one looks empty," said Max. She shaded her eyes with her hands and peered into the large enclosure.

"No, look. Over there," said Sarah.

Curled in the corner were two sleepy raccoons. Their tails were curled around them for warmth. The larger raccoon lazily opened one eye and then closed it again.

Several metres away was another pen. This time it was Max who spotted the creature inside.

"In the tree there. Up in the hollow," she said, pointing. "It's a squirrel."

When the squirrel heard the children, it hurried out of the hollow and sat up on the branch. It began chattering at them angrily, twitching its tail.

"Nothing seems wrong with that little guy," laughed Max. "Except that he's so crabby!"

Max caught sight of a bin beside the squirrel pen. She peeked in. It was empty, except for some broken peanut shells at the bottom.

She remembered Sarah's story about the shop-keeper who hadn't been paid. Would the animals be going hungry soon?

There were still more pens in the circle to look at. But just then Max heard voices. They sounded like they were coming from the other side of the clearing.

"I think that might be Abbie," Max told Sarah. "Let's go and find out."

The girls headed along the path toward the voices. As they rounded a corner, Max saw another circle of pens. In these pens were birds both big and small. In front of the pens stood Abbie and an elderly man that Max didn't recognize.

Max could hear his words: "Abbie, I was happy to come yesterday to check out the baby bobcat for you. It's so unusual to get a chance to even see one of these beautiful creatures! But I've told you before. I'm retiring from the veterinary world. My wife and I are leaving tomorrow for a long holiday. I won't be around to help out anymore."

The man put his hand on Abbie's shoulder. "My dear, you must find a place that can look after all these wild animals. And you must do it soon. Goodbye, Abbie, and good luck."

"Goodbye, Dr. Jacobs," said Abbie in a small voice. The tall woman drooped.

The vet walked back along the path toward Max and Sarah. He nodded at them sadly as he passed.

"Oh, no," said Max, after he was gone. "It sounds like the centre really is in trouble. No money and no vet. What is Abbie going to do?"

Chapter Eight

Bobcat in Disguise

Abbie wiped the tears from her eyes as Max and Sarah headed toward her.

"Max. Welcome," she said, as if nothing was wrong. Seeing Sarah, she craned her neck forward and asked, "And whooo are you?"

Max quickly introduced Sarah.

"I hope it's OK that I came with Max," Sarah said. "I . . . I just wanted to see the animals . . . "

"Oh, certainly. It's fine. Fine," Abbie insisted. She smiled kindly at Sarah, even though her eyes were still red from crying.

Max wanted to ask why Abbie was crying. She wanted to ask if Wild Paws and Claws was in trouble.

But mostly, she wanted to find out about the baby bobcat. Max blurted out, "How's Tuffy, the bobcat?"

"Tuffy is fine," Abbie said proudly. "Dr. Jacobs, our wild animal vet . . . " Abbie paused. She looked down and said slowly, "Well, he *used* to be our wild animal vet . . . "

Max and Sarah exchanged worried glances.

But then Abbie looked up and continued, "Anyway, other than losing a little weight, the little bobcat kitten is perfectly healthy." She winked at the children from behind her glasses.

Max was flooded with relief. But she still had a question. "Has Tuffy eaten? She must be hungry."

"Yes, she's eaten," Abbie reassured her. "I fed her several times last night. I used goat's milk in a small baby bottle with a nipple. As I told you, I don't know much about bobcats — and neither does Dr. Jacobs. Neither of us had ever seen one before. Bobcats just aren't too common around here. But I got your telephone message at lunchtime, and I phoned the rehabilitation centre right away. When I asked about feeding baby bobcats, the woman there was very helpful. She told me it was best to feed Tuffy with a special formula. It's for zoo animals, and it's similar to the milk of a mother bobcat. I made some up this afternoon. Tuffy loved it!"

"Maybe we could take her to Max's house and feed her," suggested Sarah. "That is, if we could borrow some of the special formula."

"Well, it's a little more complicated than that, Sarah," Abbie said kindly. "We are going to try to help Tuffy get bigger and stronger. We'll feed her formula every four hours. Then, when she's about three weeks old, we'll begin to give her some solids, such as mashed chicken." Abbie smiled at the girl. "Eventually, we hope she will be able to catch her own food. Then we'll release her back into the wild. She *is* a wild animal. She'll be happier back in the forest, free. Don't you think so?"

Sarah nodded. "I guess so," she agreed.

"So we can't let Tuffy be near too many humans. We don't want her to become used to people. We don't really want her to think that people are her friends. Although *these* people are, of course."

Abbie spread her arms to include Max, Sarah and herself in the gesture.

"But how can someone feed Tuffy without her getting used to humans?" Sarah asked, puzzled.

"Good question!" said Abbie. "The woman at the rehab centre gave me a good idea about that, too.

She recommends that while the kitten is small, whoever is feeding her should wear a bobcat mask and furred mittens. When Tuffy is bigger and she can see and smell better, the human can wear a special bobcat suit and disguise her human smell, as well."

The girls burst out laughing. "Really?" they asked.

"Really!" Abbie smiled. "When Tuffy sees or smells a person, we want her to run away! She needs to be taught how to hunt too. And then one day, perhaps next spring, Tuffy can be set free — and she'll know how to survive!"

Sarah smiled. "It sounds like a lot of work," she noted.

"But it'll be worth it," said Max firmly, thinking of Tuffy's sweet kitten face, her tightly closed eyes and her folded-back ears. Max tried to imagine her full-grown and running free in the woods. It was an exciting thought.

"So everything is fine, then," Max said with a happy sigh.

"Yes," agreed Abbie. "Everything is . . . " But she never finished her sentence. Her face crumpled. She put her hands over her face and began to cry again.

Chapter Nine

Making Plans

A short while later, Max, Sarah and Abbie were sitting in Abbie's office, drinking tea. Max was perched on a stack of books. Sarah had found a corner of the couch that wasn't piled with files and papers. Abbie had removed a few magazines from her swivel chair.

Now she opened one drawer after another in her desk. "A-ha!" she called out. She held up a packet of chocolate biscuits and offered them around.

"Tea and cookies can cheer anyone up," Abbie said brightly.

Max looked at Sarah. Then she took a deep breath and spoke. "Abbie, what's wrong? Is there anything we can do to help?"

Abbie smiled. "You're very brave to ask. I know I have been crying a lot. And I know you've seen me," she said. "I'm upset because Wild Paws and Claws must close."

She took a big gulp of tea.

"Oh, no," Max groaned. "We were right after all!"

"I wish we'd been wrong," sighed Sarah softly.

"But why does the clinic have to close?" Max asked. "What will you do with all the injured animals? Who will look after them? Who will take care of Tuffy?"

Abbie looked at Max through her round spectacles. She rubbed her thin nose.

"I've run out of money," she said simply. "I can't afford to buy food for the animals anymore. I can't really afford to buy special formula for Tuffy. And, as you know, Dr. Jacobs, who has been my volunteer vet for years, is retiring. I can't afford to pay another vet to come." She raised her palms. "So I must close the centre."

Abbie looked at the floor. "I've been resisting it, but now I have to face it. I have to find the birds and the other animals another home."

The new friends sat in silence. Their tea grew cold.

Finally Max said softly, "Abbie, if Wild Paws

and Claws wasn't here, Tuffy would have died. She would have starved."

Abbie nodded without speaking.

"You can't give up. There has to be a way to keep the centre open." Now Max's voice was a little louder and a little stronger. "Let's try to think of something."

"Yes, there has to be a way," Sarah piped up.

Abbie smiled sadly. "Really, it's wonderful that you both care so much," she said. She took her glasses off and rubbed her eyes. "But I don't think — "

"You know," Sarah said thoughtfully, twirling the ends of her braids. "I didn't even know about this centre, and I have lived in Maple Hill all my life. But when Max told me about it, I couldn't wait to come and see the animals."

Max suddenly saw what Sarah was getting at. She snapped her fingers. "Abbie, maybe you could try to get people to come and visit. I'm sure other kids and their families would want to see the furry animals and the birds if they knew Wild Paws and Claws was here!"

"You could charge them money to come," Sarah said quickly.

"That's right," Max said, nodding. "You could have a big open house! We could make posters to advertise. We could put them up in the stores and on the street posts."

"And on the posters we could write, *Save the Wild Paws and Claws clinic! Save the wild animals!*" Sarah offered. Her braids were twirling even faster now.

"We could make posters for each classroom at school," cried Max. "I'm sure all the kids would come. You could even ask for donations. We could set up a big donation box near the pens."

"We could make signs, like, *This way to the fox. This way to the raccoons.*"

"And we could write information about the animals at the centre."

"We could put their names and their information outside each pen, so people could learn more about them!"

"And we could be the tour guides — Sarah and me, and I'll bet David would help too! Abbie, you could tell us about the animal's injuries and then we could answer the visitors' questions on open house day!"

Max watched Abbie closely, and saw the hopeless look in her eyes turn hopeful. A smile played at the corners of Abbie's mouth.

"These are terrific suggestions!" she said. "And

you know, there's a little trail that circles through the woods behind the pens. I call it the Bird Trail. I have feeders set up along the path, and some swallow houses. Maybe people would find that interesting as well."

"And people would want to see Tuffy too," Sarah added. "A real bobcat!"

Abbie held up one finger. "Nope," she said firmly. "That can't be allowed. Remember, no human contact for Tuffy."

Then there was a pause.

A serious look was on Abbie's face. "It would be an awful lot of work to prepare for an open house." Abbie looked at each of the girls. "Are you sure you want to help? You'd have to come every day after school – and on the weekend too. Are you sure you have time?"

"We're sure!" Max answered at once. "Right, Sarah?"

"Yes," Sarah agreed, nodding her head fiercely.

"And I know David will want to help too. I know it!" Max added.

"Well, OK!" Abbie said, clapping her hands with delight. "So let's get busy." Abbie put her glasses back on and opened her calendar. "We have a lot to do. Paper, markers, pens and tape to buy.

But first, we need to choose a day for the open house. And it needs to be soon, because the money is almost all gone . . . "

When that was done, it was almost time to go.

But suddenly Max spoke up. In a small voice she asked, "Abbie, is there any way I can help with Tuffy? Is there any way I can help without harming her? Even if I could just take a peek at her . . . "

Abbie smiled at the girl. She reached out and touched her arm.

"Oh, you poor dear. How thoughtless of me. Come on."

Max saw Sarah looking at her longingly.

"Abbie, could Sarah come too? She hasn't had a chance to see the bobcat yet."

Abbie hesitated. "OK," she said finally. "Since Tuffy can't see or hear yet."

The friends eagerly followed the tall woman outside. She led them to a small room attached to the back of the office.

"This is the isolation room," Abbie explained. "It's warm here and soundproof. That way Tuffy can be near the office, but she won't get used to hearing human voices."

They went into the room. On a table against the back wall was a small pet carrier.

Abbie unlatched the door to the carrier. Max held her breath. She and Sarah peered inside.

There was tiny Tuffy, sleeping soundly.

"I fed Tuffy right before you came," Abbie told the girls.

The bobcat had a contented look on her sweet face. Her white whiskers twitched in her dreams. Tuffy's little belly was full of formula.

Max noticed that Tuffy was resting on a pad that half covered the bottom of the cage.

"That's a heating pad," Abbie explained. "Newborns need to stay warm. It's really important that Tuffy has a heated place where she can lie down if she needs to warm up. If she gets too warm, she can just move off it."

"Oh, she's so sweet!" breathed Sarah. "She's so tiny!"

"She looks like a little ball of fur," whispered Max.

Max thought of finding Tuffy alone in the rocks. She remembered her sad mewing. She remembered how the baby bobcat had lifted her head and searched helplessly for milk. Now Tuffy was safe and cared for.

"She looks very happy." Max sighed and smiled.

Abbie looked hard at the girl. "Max, I've been

thinking. I know how much you care about the little bobcat. And I know I'm going to need some help. When you come tomorrow, Max, you can do the feeding. I'll teach you how. And then after that, you can feed her any time you're here and she's hungry."

Max's round eyes met Abbie's. "Really?" she asked. "Are you sure it would be OK?"

Abbie nodded. "I'm positive. Oh, and bring an old teddy bear that you don't mind putting in the carrier. Bobcat kittens like to snuggle. Just ask your mom to put it through the washer and dryer tonight."

Max swallowed hard. She could hardly wait for tomorrow to come. She could hardly wait for the work ahead — feeding a baby bobcat and, with her new friend, organizing an open house to keep Wild Paws and Claws open!

Chapter Ten

Hard Work

The next day after school, Max, Sarah and David ran straight to Wild Paws and Claws, ready to work.

"I could hardly breathe while my mother talked to Abbie on the phone!" Max told Sarah as they walked down the clinic's driveway. "Finally, Mom hung up and told me that Abbie sounded wonderful. She said I could help with feeding Tuffy."

"Max almost cried," added David.

Max dug her elbow into her brother's side. "Hey, if you want to help with the open house, you can't be a pest," she said.

"OK, OK," he promised with a grin.

Just then Max caught sight of Abbie coming from the pens.

"Hi!" Abbie called. She was wearing gloves and a heavy jacket that was too short for her tall body. Her black rubber boots were up to her knees and almost as long as they were tall. A yellow bucket dangled from her hand.

"I've just fed Tippy the fox and Nutcracker the squirrel. But I haven't fed Tuffy yet, Max," Abbie said. She scratched her long, thin nose as she talked. "I'll show you kids around the office, and then we can take care of that little bobcat. OK?"

"Great!" Max cried.

Abbie led the way into the office building. She pointed out her many books about wildlife and told the kids they could use her computer. She showed them the Bristol board, markers and other drawing materials that she had bought.

Max and Sarah began to divide up the jobs.

"How about you make some posters?" Max suggested to David. "The sooner we begin advertising for the open house, the better."

"I'll start making signs for the pens," decided Sarah.

"And I'll give you a hand when we're done with Tuffy," Max promised.

Max picked up the teddy bear that she had brought for Tuffy, and Abbie took a bag of supplies. They headed over to the isolation room.

"I was thinking about what the woman at the bobcat rehab centre told me," said Abbie. "About how important it is that Tuffy keeps her natural fear of humans. So I went to the fabric store this morning."

Abbie handed Max a hood and a pair of furry mittens.

"Wow!" exclaimed Max. "The material looks just like the coat of a bobcat! The hood looks like Tuffy's head, except it has holes for eyes and the ears are standing straight up!"

"I bought enough of this fur-like material to make two masks and two pairs of mittens – one large set and one small set – and two full-body suits. I didn't have enough time to sew the suits," Abbie said, putting on the larger mask, "but I thought we should wear the mask and mittens right away. One day soon, Tuffy is going to open her eyes!"

Max eagerly put on the mask. Then she slipped on the soft mittens that Abbie handed her.

"Oops! One more thing," Abbie said as they reached the isolation room door. "It's important that we disguise our human smell, and it's a good idea to use something from the bobcat's wild environment. So here we go – pine needles!"

Max and Abbie rubbed the pine needles on the mittens, on their arms and pants and on the old, worn teddy bear.

Then Max looked up at Abbie, trying not to seem too impatient. "Now?" she asked. "Are we ready now?"

Abbie nodded, with a sympathetic smile. "Ready. Just remember – no talking. I don't think Tuffy can hear yet. But we don't know when those ears are going to start working, and we don't want Tuffy to get to like our voices, either!"

Abbie began to open the door, and then she paused. "Oh, and Max, when we go inside, just unlock the cage and gently lift Tuffy out. Hold her just the way you'd hold a kitten. Be careful – she might be squirmy!"

Finally, the door was open, and Max stepped inside. Right away she heard Tuffy mewing. The kitten was hungry!

Chapter Eleven

What If...?

Max hurried right over to Tuffy's carrier cage. Her heart pounding, Max reached down with her furry mittens and gently picked up the bobcat kitten. She *was* squirmy! Oh, did it feel wonderful to hold that little body in her arms again!

In a moment, Abbie came over with a small bottle in her hand. She motioned to the floor. Max nodded, understanding. Carefully she sat down, crossing her legs and holding Tuffy safely in her lap.

Abbie handed the bottle of formula to Max. Silently, she showed Max how to feed Tuffy with it. Then she let her do it herself.

The little bobcat kitten couldn't see the bottle,

but she could certainly smell the formula! She reached out with her tiny paws and searched for the nipple with her nose.

Max smiled as Tuffy began to drink eagerly. The kitten's eyes were squeezed shut. Her ears were flat against her head.

Several minutes passed, and then Tuffy stopped drinking. The milk was gone. Tuffy had finished the whole bottle!

Max smiled. The kitten lay happily in her lap. Max looked at Tuffy's little whitish belly. It looked plump and full. Max sighed contentedly, gazing down at Tuffy.

Then, an amazing thing happened. Max noticed the kitten's face scrunching up again. She began arching her eyebrows.

Max waited expectantly. What was she doing?

Suddenly, Tuffy's eyes were opening! They didn't open wide. They were like two little slits. But they were definitely open – and the most beautiful shade of deep blue.

And then, the kitten's tiny face seemed to turn to Max. Her eyes seemed to look right into Max's eyes.

Max felt a surge of joy.

This little wild animal didn't have a mother anymore. But she had Max now – and Abbie and

Sarah. Tuffy was alive, and she was healthy, and she was tough. She was going to be just fine.

All too soon, Abbie returned. Max knew it was time to put Tuffy back in the carrier.

Oh, the teddy bear for Tuffy! Max silently remembered. She placed it inside with the bobcat. Tummy full, the tiny kitten curled up against the teddy bear's leg, and as Max watched, she fell happily to sleep.

When Max and Abbie returned to the office, Max told the others that Tuffy had opened her eyes for the first time.

"That means she must be about two weeks old,"

Max concluded. She decided right away to make an information sheet about Tuffy. "Guests to the centre can't meet Tuffy, because she'll be in the isolation room. But they'll be fascinated to know that she's here. And they'll want to know all about bobcats! Don't you think?"

Sarah and David agreed wholeheartedly.

Max began by making notes on everything she already knew about bobcats. Then she did some more research, using Abbie's books.

The time flew by. David finally lifted up his poster. "Here. I've finished the first one. What do you think?"

The poster was big and colourful. It had drawings of a fox, a rabbit and a squirrel on it. There were speech balloons coming out of their mouths. They were saying, *Help!!! Come and visit us. You can find us at the Wild Paws and Claws Clinic and Rehabilitation Centre.*

David had even drawn a map showing the location of the centre. He also had the date of the open house and the admission fee.

"That's great!" cried Max enthusiastically.

The children bent their heads down and returned to their work. Then Abbie suddenly looked at her watch.

"Oh, my goodness," she said, putting her hand up to her mouth. "It's almost your dinnertime, kids! Please give your parents a call, and tell them I'll drive you home tonight," Abbie offered. "I didn't realize it was so late!"

"Neither did we," said Max. She had just put the finishing touches on the bobcat information sheet.

Everyone hurriedly tidied up and they all jumped in Abbie's car. Abbie dropped off Sarah first and then Max and David. Max waved goodbye to Abbie as she and her brother hurried in the front door.

Grandma, Mom and Dad were already eating dinner.

"Hi! Sorry we're late," called Max, as she ran to wash her hands.

David was first to sit down. Right away, he began to share what they had done that afternoon. "Sarah and Abbie wrote up two information sheets," he reported excitedly. "One was for Nutcracker, the blind squirrel. And the other one was for Tippy the fox. He's called Tippy because he has white on the tip of his tail. Abbie says Tippy can't be released back into the wild."

"Uh-oh. Why not?" asked Dad.

"Tippy was injured when he was a kit," replied

David. His forkful of spaghetti was halfway to his mouth. "He never learned how to find his own food. And guess what else we did?"

"You take a bite, and I'll tell," suggested Max. "I wrote an information sheet about Tuffy, and David made two posters to advertise the open house."

"Terrific!" said Mom proudly.

Dad had a suggestion. "How about I put up one of the posters on my way through town tomorrow?"

"And I'll walk over to the library and put the other one up," chimed in Grandma.

"That would be great," said David. "I'm going to make more tomorrow afternoon. I'm going to make some for the school too."

"Soon everyone will know about the open house at Wild Paws and Claws!" said Max.

But as she chewed her spaghetti, she couldn't help worrying. Soon everyone would know about the open house. But what if no one came? What if they didn't raise enough money to save Wild Paws and Claws? What would happen to all the animals . . . and Tuffy?

Chapter Twelve

Open House Day

"I can't believe it's really Saturday," said Sarah nervously. "The day of the open house." She finished taping up the last sign: *This way to the Bird Trail*.

"Me neither," said Max with a smile. "But I think everything is just about set." She had just filled all the bird feeders on the trail. She was trying to sound confident. She knew they had worked hard and they were ready. They were going to do their best.

"The thought of leading a tour gives me butterflies in my stomach," Sarah confided to Max as they headed back to the office.

"Me too," agreed Max. The girls smiled at each other.

"But we have to do it," Max shrugged.

"Yes," Sarah agreed. "We just have to show the visitors how much their help is needed here."

Abbie was stationed in the parking lot. David was standing at the office door. He impatiently glanced at his watch.

"The open house began at 10 am," he pointed out, "and it's 10:01. There aren't any visitors yet!"

Max and Sarah burst out giggling.

"David, don't worry," Max said. "Just be patient."

But even as she spoke, a blue car pulled into the parking lot. Max watched a family of five jump out, then saw another family walking down the lane toward them.

"Here we go, gang!" Abbie called, waving her hand. "It's time for action!"

The three kids tied on their orange armbands. These would identify them as tour guides. They watched as Abbie smiled and chatted, accepting money and giving out tickets.

"Me first! Me first!" begged David as the visitors approached. Max watched as her brother headed over to them with the words, "May I help you? Would you like a tour?"

Moments later another family arrived. Sarah took a deep breath.

"Good luck. I'm sure you'll do fine," Max told her.

Sarah gave her a wobbly smile and hurried away to show the visitors around the centre.

Then Max watched as a station wagon unloaded six of her classmates. And then six more piled out of a brown van. A small group formed.

Max was the only tour guide available, so she marched over to help out.

"Welcome to Wild Paws and Claws. I am Max and I am going to be your tour guide," she said. Her classmates all cheered. "Follow me," she told them, and her first tour began.

The day went by quickly. Max discovered that she really enjoyed giving the tours. The visitors were very interested in seeing the furry animals and the birds. They listened to Max's information about each one. And they asked lots of questions.

When she couldn't answer a question, Max said, "I'll try and find out the answer. I'll have it ready for the next time you come."

Toward the end of the day, David suddenly called, "Mom! Dad! Grandma!"

Max and David raced to greet them.

"What's first?" Mom asked.

Max led them over to the isolation room. On the door was an information sheet and photographs.

"Tuffy is in here," Max said.

"Oh, look! You took some photos!" Mom said. "Now everyone can see what Tuffy actually looks like. What a wonderful idea!"

Max pointed out the photo taken on the first day. There was Tuffy, tiny and hungry. Every other day, Max had taken a picture. Before their eyes, the little bobcat kitten grew, becoming bigger and healthier in each photo.

"Her fur looks so soft!" exclaimed Dad.

"And look – her eyes are open here," Mom pointed out.

"Yes, and can you see how her ears have started to unfold here?" Max added.

"Oh, they have little tufts on them!" Mom said. "And what an adorable tail. It's a bobtail, I guess!"

Everyone read and admired the notes that Max had made.

"Now this way!" announced David.

Max and David happily led their family to the pens. They showed them the birds and then the

other animals. Everyone stopped and read each handmade information sheet.

By the time the Kearney family had gone around the Bird Trail, it was late afternoon.

As they headed back to the office, David looked at his watch. "Open house is officially over," he reported.

Max gulped.

How much money had they raised? Would it be enough to carry on?

Then Max saw them – Sarah and Abbie, sitting together on the front steps. Max's heart lurched.

Sarah had an arm on Abbie's shoulder, and Abbie had her face in her hands. Was Abbie crying again?

Oh, no! Max knew it could only mean one thing. Disaster!

Chapter Thirteen

Bobcat Wild

"What's wrong?" called Max nervously. She looked at Abbie's wet face. But, to her surprise, Abbie was smiling through her tears.

"Nothing's wrong," said Sarah with a grin.

"I cry when I'm sad. But I cry when I'm happy, too!" Abbie said cheerfully. She wiped the tears from her face and gave the surprised Max a quick hug.

She smiled at Mom, Dad and Grandma. "You must belong to Max and David," she said. "It's very nice to meet you. You have wonderful children," she told them.

Before they had a chance to reply, Abbie went on. "I have very good news!" she exclaimed. "I haven't counted up all the money yet, but we made lots on admissions today. And I took a peek in the donation box. It's almost overflowing. I am sure there is enough money to keep Wild Paws and Claws going — at least until our next open house!"

Max threw her arms around Abbie. "Oh, I'm so glad!" she cried. "None of the animals have to leave. And we can keep Tuffy. We have time to teach her how to look after herself. Then one day maybe we can release her!"

Sarah joined in the hug, and David did too.

Abbie stood up, finally, wiping her eyes again.

Then she shook her finger at Sarah and Max, trying to look stern. "But don't think you're off the hook, you two," she said. "Just because we have a little money, it doesn't mean I don't still need you."

Max and Sarah looked at Abbie hopefully.

"I'll need some helpers one or two afternoons a week. You know, to help feed the animals and fill the bird feeders. And I thought we could open to the public for a few hours every Saturday afternoon. That might keep some money coming in."

The children held their breath.

"And every time a new animal comes, there will be another information sheet to write. And I thought we could have a special day when school-children can come at half price," Abbie went on.

Max's eyes opened wide.

"And I will need some tour guides. And of course I'll need Max to keep helping me to care for Tuffy. So you see, there will be lots more work than I can handle all on my own . . . "

She peered at the children through her round glasses. "Well?" she asked impatiently. "Will you help me?"

"Yes!" shouted Max and Sarah as loudly as they could. "We will!"

Finally the exciting day was over. It was time for everyone to go home.

But Max wasn't quite ready to go yet. She looked at Abbie.

"Can I just go and see Tuffy one last time before we leave? Please? I promise I won't disturb her."

Abbie nodded, and Max's parents agreed to wait.

Max went alone into the isolation room. She slipped on the mask and the mittens, but Tuffy didn't see her or smell her. The baby bobcat was sound asleep. For a long moment, Max stood gazing down at the little spotted body. She admired the kitten's tiny orange nose, her white whiskers and her dainty mouth. She watched her belly rise and fall. Tuffy twitched once, and Max wondered if she was having a happy dream. Maybe a dream about her days in the rocky den with her mother and sibling. Or maybe a dream about her new foster moms.

Max smiled. She spoke to the little bobcat in her thoughts: You're going to be all right, Tuffy. We're going to make sure of that. And one day – one day soon – you're going to be free again!

Bobcat Information Sheet

❖ Bobcats are wild cats. They are related to the lynx and the cougar, other North American wild cats.

❖ Bobcats are curious, but very shy. They are rarely seen by humans, and they never approach people. They live in a variety of habitats – from forests to grassy areas. They like rocky areas where they can shelter and raise their young. Bobcats cannot move easily through deep snow, which is why they only live as far north as southern Canada.

❖ Bobcats are carnivorous, eating only meat. They usually eat small birds or other animals, such as rabbits, hares and mice. They will also eat deer, rattlesnakes, flying squirrels, fish, snails and insects.

❖ When hunting, a bobcat may stalk its prey until it is close enough to strike. Or the bobcat may hide or wait by the burrow of a small mammal for as long as 45 minutes. When its prey appears, it will leap out and ambush it.

❧ An adult bobcat is about twice the size of a domestic cat. It has a tawny brown coat — reddish in summer and greyish in winter — with many black spots. Its tawny legs have black horizontal bars. The bobcat has a streaked ruff on each cheek. Its pointy ears are tufted and tipped with black.

❧ The short tail of the bobcat is tipped with black and is white underneath. This colouring can come in handy for a mother bobcat. When her kittens are falling behind, she stops and wags her tail. Her kittens see the white signal — and they hurry to catch up!

❧ Bobcats live alone, except when the female is raising her young. The male bobcat does not help with the parenting. Bobcats strike out on their own at about nine to ten months of age.

❧ The bobcat has a piercing scream. When it is threatened, it makes a short, sudden "cough-bark."